Nate the Great
Goes Undercover

Nate the Great
Goes Undercover

by Marjorie Weinman Sharmat
illustrated by Marc Simont

A YEARLING BOOK

All rights reserved. Published in the United States by Yearling, an imprint of Random House Children's Books, a division of Penguin Random House LLC, New York. Originally published in hardcover in the United States by Coward-McCann in 1974. Subsequently published in paperback by Yearling in 1978, and reissued with Extra Fun Activities, in 2006. Reprinted by arrangement with the Putnam and Grosset Group.

Yearling and the jumping horse design are registered trademarks of Penguin Random House LLC.

Visit us on the Web! randomhousekids.com

Educators and librarians, for a variety of teaching tools, visit us at RHTeachersLibrarians.com

Library of Congress Cataloging-in-Publication Data is available upon request.
ISBN 978-0-440-46302-3 (pbk.) — ISBN 978-0-385-37679-2 (ebook)

Printed in the United States of America
76   75   74   73   72
First Yearling Edition 1978

Random House Children's Books supports the First Amendment and celebrates the right to read.

For my wonderful father, Nate

I, Nate the Great, am a detective.

I work hard,

I rest hard.

Tonight I am resting hard

from my last case.

It was my first night case.

It started in the morning
before breakfast.

I was walking my dog, Sludge.

Sludge is my new dog.

I found him in a field
eating a stale pancake.

I love pancakes.

I knew he was my kind of dog.

I saw Oliver come
out of his house.

Oliver lives next door.

Sludge and I walked faster.

Oliver walked faster.

Oliver caught up with us.

He always catches up with us.

Oliver is a pest.

"There is a garbage snatcher
in the neighborhood," Oliver said.
"Our can is tipped over
every night.
I need help."
Oliver knows I am a detective.
He knows I am a good detective.

"I will help you," I said.
"I, Nate the Great,
will help you
pick up your garbage."
"That is not the kind of help
I need," Oliver said.
"I want to know who is taking
the garbage every night."

"That is easy," I said.

"Somebody hungry

is taking your garbage.

Somebody very hungry.

And sleepy.

Somebody sleepy

from getting up every night

to take your garbage."

"Do you know anybody

hungry and sleepy?" Oliver asked.

"Yes," I said. "Me.

I will find the garbage snatcher

after I eat breakfast."

Sludge and I went home.

I cooked a giant pancake.

I gave some to Sludge.

Then we went outside.

I said to Sludge,

"I'll ask questions

while you sniff. If you sniff any

garbage smells, let me know."

I saw Rosamond coming

down the street with her cats.

Rosamond did not look
hungry or sleepy.
She looked like she always looks.
Strange.

Sludge sniffed while I spoke.

"Rosamond, do you eat garbage?"

Rosamond said, "There are

two thousand other things

I would eat

before I would eat garbage.

First, I would eat hamburger,

ice cream, candy, pickles, bananas,

potato chips, Krispy Krappies,

relish, doughnuts, spaghetti,

ice cubes, mint leaves. . . ."

Rosamond kept talking.

I did not have time

to hear her list

of two thousand things.

I walked on.

Rosamond was still talking.
"Pretzels, artichokes,
baked beans, chocolate pudding,
vegetable soup, walnuts . . ."
Rosamond had two thousand
reasons for not
taking Oliver's garbage.
But what about her cats?

I went back to Rosamond.

"Cauliflower, wafers, lamb chops,"
she said. "Peanuts, egg salad . . ."

"Excuse me," I said.

"Do your cats eat garbage?"

"No," Rosamond said. "My cats
eat cat food, cheese, tuna fish,
milk, salmon pie, liver loaf. . . ."

I walked away.

I decided to look for Esmeralda.
Esmeralda always has
her mouth open.
She is either hungry
or about to yawn.
I saw her sitting
in front of her house.
Sludge sniffed. I spoke.
"Do you get up at night to visit
Oliver's garbage can?" I asked.
"I would never visit anything
that belongs to Oliver,"
Esmeralda said.
"He might follow me."
Now I knew why Esmeralda
keeps her mouth open.

She has wise things to say.

She had given me

an important clue.

No person would go near

Oliver or his garbage.

Oliver is too much of a pest.

Sludge and I went home.

Oliver came over.

Oliver always comes over.

Sludge sniffed Oliver.

I gave Sludge a pancake.

"Is the case solved?" Oliver asked.

"Part of it," I said.

"Which part?" he asked.

"I, Nate the Great, have found out

who did *not* take your garbage.

A person did not

take your garbage."

"Well, who took it?" Oliver asked.

"That is the part

that is not solved," I said.

"I, Nate the Great, say

that an animal or bird took it.

An animal or bird that goes out

in the night. I will find out what

and I will be back."

Sometimes I, Nate the Great,

need help.

I went to the library.

I read about birds that

go out in the night.

They are called Strigiformes

and Caprimulgiformes.

I wrote the names down.

Then I crossed them out.

Birds with names like that

would not eat anything
called garbage.
Then I read about cats, rats, bats,
mice, shrews, skunks, raccoons,
opossums, and moles.
They all go out at night.

I read about what they like
and what they do not like.
Then I went home.
Oliver came over.
I said, "A cat, rat, bat, mouse,
shrew, skunk, raccoon, opossum,
or mole is taking your garbage."

"Which one?" Oliver asked.

"I don't know. But tonight,

I, Nate the Great, will find out."

I left a note for my mother.

Dear mother,
I am sleeping out tonight.
I am taking a blanket.
I am taking pancakes.
I will be back.
Love,
Nate the Great

I went out into the yard.

It was cold out there.

I asked Sludge if I could share

his doghouse.

I crawled in.

Sludge crawled out.

It was a small doghouse.
I looked out the window
of the doghouse.
I could not see
Oliver's garbage can.
I crawled out of the doghouse.
I left Sludge a pancake.

Where could I hide?
I, Nate the Great,
knew where to hide.
In the garbage can.
I was sorry I knew.
Detective work is not
fun and games.

Detective work is dirty garbage
cans instead of clean beds.
Detective work is banana peels,
dishrags, milk cartons, floor
sweepings, cigar ashes, fleas,
and me
all together in one can.

I peeked out
from under the cover.
The street was quiet.
Then I heard a sound.
Crunch! Crackle! Klunk!
The sound was close to me.
The sound was me.

The garbage can was crunchy

and crackly and klunky.

Every time I moved

it was crunchier and cracklier.

I lifted up the cover. I got out.

I had a new plan. A better plan.

I would not wait

for the garbage snatcher.

I would go out and find him.

I crept down the street.

I looked to the right

and to the left

and behind me.

Right, left, behind.

Right, left, behind.

Smack!

Something big hit me.

It was in front of me.

The one place I forgot to look.

I do not think

I made a dent

in the telephone pole.

I kept creeping and looking.

Right, left, behind, front.

Right, left, behind, front.

I came to a field.

Animals like fields.

I saw an animal.

I, Nate the Great, was in luck.

I crept closer.

I, Nate the Great, was in bad luck.

It was a skunk.

I started to walk backward.

I saw some stuff on the ground
next to the skunk.

It looked like garbage.

I walked forward to see.

I saw some garbage.

The skunk saw me.

The skunk stamped his feet.

He raised his tail.

I, Nate the Great,

did not run fast enough.

But the case was solved.

The skunk

was the garbage snatcher.

I went home.

I wrote a note to Oliver.

I put it in his mailbox.

Dear Oliver,
I, Nate the great, have found out
who took your garbage.
It was a skunk.
I, Nate the great,
know how to get rid of
a skunk.
Put a can of mothballs
next to your garbage can.
Skunks do not like the smell of
mothballs.
I learned this in the Library.
I do not like the smell of skunk.
I learned this in the field.
Yours truly,
Nate the great

It was not morning yet.

But I knew there was something

I must do

right away.

I was glad the water was hot.

In fact, that is how

I spent most of the next day.

The following morning
Oliver came over.
"The case is unsolved," he said.
"The garbage can is tipped again."
"Impossible," I said.
"Come and see my
garbage," Oliver said.
I, Nate the Great, have had
better invitations.

But I went.

The can was tipped, all right.

"And here is the can of mothballs,"
Oliver said. "So who is
the garbage snatcher?" he asked.
"I, Nate the Great, will find out,
no matter how long
or how many baths it takes."

I walked away.

Sludge followed me.

He was doing a lot of sniffing.

But I, Nate the Great,

had a lot of thinking to do.

I gave Sludge a pancake.

There must be a clue I missed.

Sludge ignored the pancake.

He was thinking, too.

I thought harder.

And harder.

Then I knew what the clue was.

All I needed was the proof.

I left a note for my mother.

Dear mother,
I will be nextdoor Tonight.
I will have a cover.
I will be back.
Love,
Nate the Great

I went to the garbage can.

I stepped inside.

I put the cover over me.

I left space to look out

and to breathe.

I knew that was important.

I waited.

Nothing happened.

Something came up to the can.

Something knocked
the cover to the ground.

Something looked inside.

"Something" was Sludge.

Sludge was surprised to see me.

But I, Nate the Great, had been

expecting to see Sludge.

I knew that Sludge

was the garbage snatcher.

And I knew why.

Sludge was tired of my pancakes.

How could anybody

be tired of pancakes?

Sludge was looking

for his own snack.

Sludge was hungry.

I took him back to his doghouse.

I gave him a bone

and a bowl of dog food.

Someday Sludge

will be a great detective,

when he learns to sniff more

and snatch less.

I wanted to take a bath.

But I was too tired.

I wanted to write a note to Oliver.

But I was too tired.

Tomorrow Oliver will come over.

Oliver always comes over.

Now I am resting.

I can hear the sounds of the night.

I can hear the sounds of a

crunchy bone being crunched.

They are good sounds.

My first night case is over.

Maybe it will be my last night case.

I, Nate the Great, am pooped.

~Extra~ Fun Activities!

What's Inside

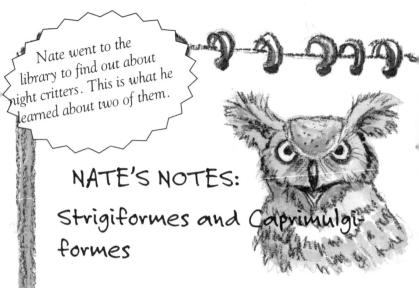

Nate went to the library to find out about night critters. This is what he learned about two of them.

NATE'S NOTES:

Strigiformes and Caprimulgiformes

STRIGIFORMES is a fancy name for owls.

Owls would make good detectives. They fly silently. They have excellent hearing. They can turn their heads so far that they can almost see behind themselves! Like detectives, they say, "Who? Who?"

Owls are raptors. That means they are birds that eat meat. They have eight sharp talons, and hooked beaks. Their heads are round. They catch mice, voles, and birds by listening to the tiny noises the animals make in the forest.

Owls usually tear their prey into large pieces. Sometimes they swallow it whole. They later cough up pellets of undigested bones, fur, scales, and feathers. These pellets are found under their nests.

Owls are mainly nocturnal. About 145 different species frequent the night skies. The smallest owl in the United States, the elf owl, measures six inches. The largest, the great gray owl, grows to about two and a half feet tall.

CAPRIMULGIFORMES is another name for nightjars. What's a nightjar? It's a jay-sized bird that nests on the ground. The males make a distinctive chirring noise.

Like owls, nightjars fly silently. Unlike owls, they fly with their mouths wide open. This helps them snatch insects, like moths, out of the air.

Nightjars are sometimes called masters of disguise. That's because their dull feathers blend in with their surroundings and hide them during the day. The secretive birds won't fly away until you almost step on them.

WEIRD FACT: Nightjars are more active when the moon is full.

One nightjar found in the United States is the common nighthawk. It nests in forest clearings, in vacant lots, and even on flat roofs. Nighthawks are good neighbors: they can gobble up five hundred mosquitoes in one day.

NATE'S NOTES:

Creatures of the Night

On this case, some of Nate's suspects were night critters. Here are some things to know about creatures that prowl the night while you're snug in bed:

CATS like to hunt mice at night. An excellent sense of smell helps them. A cat's OLFACTORY MEMBRANE—the part of the nose that detects smells—is about three times bigger than a human's. If they can't hunt, house cats will sometimes pounce on their sleeping owners instead.

RATS will eat just about anything: garbage, pet food, dropped fruit—even dog poop! They can find food by feeling around in the dark with their whiskers.

BATS can catch flying insects in the dark! That's because bats "see" by making high-pitched noises and listening for the echoes to bounce back. This specialized hearing is called ECHOLOCATION.

MICE have big eyes. This helps them see well in the dark because big eyes can collect more light.

SHREWS slink out after dark to gobble up huge amounts of moth and beetle larvae, earthworms, and spiders. They must eat about half of their body weight each day, or starve. Their favorite hunting tool? Bristly whiskers around their mouth that help them feel out their prey in the dark.

SKUNKS are generally found foraging around midnight. Looking for food late at night helps them avoid predators like dogs, coyotes, and badgers.

Do you hear strange bumps in the night? RACCOONS have nimble fingers that allow them to climb through pet doors and open refrigerators. They can also climb down trees headfirst.

Day or night, an attacked OPOSSUM (or POSSUM) will "play possum." The animal goes stiff, its eyes glaze over, and its tongue hangs out of its mouth. Many predators will leave the possum alone if they believe it is already dead. An opossum can play dead as long as four hours.

Many people think MOLES are nocturnal because they wake up to find mole-dug tunnels across their yard. Actually, moles conduct this tunneling activity day and night. To assist them, they have oversized front paws with sharp claws, which allow them to dig 12 to 15 feet per hour.

13

How to Make Rosamond's Favorite Food: Hamburgers

Rosamond is not weird when it comes to her favorite food. Hamburgers are pretty normal. On average, Americans eat about three each week!

Ask an adult to help you with this recipe. It will make four burgers.

GET TOGETHER:

- $\frac{1}{4}$ cup of milk
- a small sauté pan
- one slice of white bread
- a mixing bowl
- 1 egg
- $\frac{1}{2}$ teaspoon of salt
- a dash of ground pepper

- 1 pound of ground beef
- additional seasonings such as garlic powder, onion powder, dried basil, and chili powder (if you want some)
- a large frying pan
- a spatula
- 4 hamburger buns
- ketchup, mustard, mayonnaise, relish, pickles, tomato slices, lettuce, spinach leaves, onion slices—whatever toppings you like!

HOW TO MAKE YOUR HAMBURGERS:

1. Add the milk to the sauté pan. Warm over low heat. Remove from heat. Tear the bread into small pieces and put them in the milk. Allow to cool.

2. Transfer the milk-bread mixture to the mixing bowl. Add the egg, salt, pepper, and ground beef, plus a pinch of any other seasonings you're trying.

3. Mix everything together with your fingers. Form the mixture into four equal-sized patties.

4. Place the frying pan over medium-high heat. After a few minutes, add the patties.
5. Cook the patties for five minutes; then flip them. Cook them for five minutes on the other side.
6. Place each burger on a bun. Add toppings of your choice. Eat!

Funny Pages

What do you call a great dog detective?
Sherlock Bones!

Where should you never take a dog?
A *flea market.*

Why did the dalmatian go to the eye doctor?
He kept seeing spots.

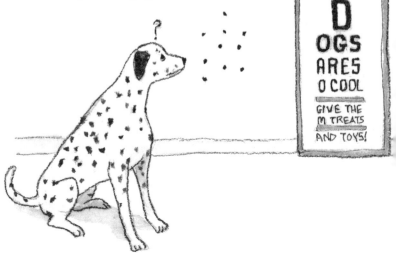

What did the dog do at the library?
He boned up on his favorite subject.

How does a dog stop a VCR?
He hits the "paws" button.

What do you call a sick dog?
A germy shepherd!

How to Make Rosamond's Second-Favorite Food: Ice Cream

Ice cream is Rosamond's second-favorite food. Hasn't she heard of pancakes? In case you like ice cream too, here's a recipe.

Makes about a pint.

GET TOGETHER:

- 1 egg
- a fork
- 2 cups of cream
- $\frac{1}{2}$ cup of sugar
- 1 teaspoon of vanilla extract
- a large spoon
- a small storage container with a tight-fitting lid.* All the ingredients above should fit inside with a little extra room.

Tupperware or Lock & Lock works well. You can also use a Ziploc bag.

- masking tape
- a big plastic storage container with a lid. The small container should easily fit inside. Round is best.
- 6 cups of ice
- 1 cup of rock salt (from the grocery or hardware store)
- a towel
- add-ins (if you want them): chocolate chips, nuts, sprinkles, chopped peppermints, chopped candy bars, or whatever you like

MAKE YOUR ICE CREAM:

1. Crack the egg into the small container. Beat well with the fork.
2. Add the cream, sugar, and vanilla. Mix well with the spoon.
3. Put the lid on the small container. Tape around the lid to make sure salt doesn't get inside. Place in the large container.

4. Pack 2 cups of the ice and $\frac{1}{3}$ cup of the rock salt around the small container. If there is room in your container, add another 2 cups of ice and $\frac{1}{3}$ cup of salt. Repeat with the rest of the ice and salt if there is room. Don't worry if all the ice and salt won't fit.
5. Put the lid on the large container.
6. Roll the large container back and forth on the towel for about fifteen minutes. Or repeatedly flip a bag or square container.

7. Open the large container and remove the smaller one. Wipe it clean.
8. Open the small container and stir in any add-ins.
9. Close the small container. Return it to the large container. Roll or flip for another ten minutes.
10. Open the large container. Dump the ice and salt.
11. Wipe the small container and open it. Eat!

More Funny Pages

Why did the dog jump into the river?
He was chasing a catfish!

What do you say to a dog before he eats?
Bone appétit!

What kind of dog can jump higher than
a building?
Any dog! Buildings can't jump.

What do you call a dog that gets mail?
A golden receiver!

What kind of dog is the quietest?
A hush puppy!

Where does a dog go if it loses its tail?
To a retail store.

YOUR CHOICE

How to Have a Good Long Soak

Nate met a skunk and needed a good long soak. Try these tricks and maybe your next bath won't seem so long.

1. Add a drop or two of food coloring to the water. Turn your bath as blue as a lagoon. Or as red as clay. Try mixing different colors to create a new hue.*

2. Fill four cups with white shaving cream. Stir in a few drops of food coloring. Use the "paint" to decorate the bath or yourself. Pink knees, anyone?*

*Ask an adult first. Make sure the dye won't stain your tub or tile.

3. Freeze small toys in ice-cube trays and add the cubes to your bathwater. Pretend to be an archaeologist discovering ancient artifacts.

4. If you are itchy or sunburned, add two cups of apple cider vinegar to the water. The vinegar will soothe your skin.

5. Add a big scoop of salt and an equal amount of baking soda to your bathwater. Pretend you're in a hot mineral spring.

A word about learning with

Nate the Great

The Nate the Great series is good fun and has been entertaining children for over forty years. These books are also valuable learning tools in and out of the classroom.

Nate's world—his home, his friends, his neighborhood—is one that every young person recognizes. Nate introduces beginning readers and those who have graduated to early chapter books to the detective mystery genre, and they respond to Nate's commitment to solving the case and helping his friends.

What's more, as Nate the Great solves his cases, readers learn with him. Nate unravels mysteries by using evidence collection, cogent reasoning, problem-solving, analytical skills, and logic in a way that teaches readers to develop critical-thinking abilities. The stories help children start discussions about how to approach difficult situations and give them tools to resolve them.

When you read a Nate the Great book with a child, or when a child reads a Nate the Great mystery on his or her own, the child is guaranteed a satisfying ending that will have taught him or her important classroom and life skills. We know that you and your children will enjoy reading and learning from Nate the Great's wonderful stories as much as we do.

Find out more at NatetheGreatBooks.com.

Happy reading and learning with Nate!

Solve all the mysteries with

Nate the Great

- Nate the Great and the Crunchy Christmas
- Nate the Great Saves the King of Sweden
- Nate the Great and Me: The Case of the Fleeing Fang
- Nate the Great and the Monster Mess
- Nate the Great, San Francisco Detective
- Nate the Great and the Big Sniff
- Nate the Great on the Owl Express
- Nate the Great Talks Turkey
- Nate the Great and the Hungry Book Club
- Nate the Great, Where Are You?

MARJORIE WEINMAN SHARMAT has written more than 130 books for children and young adults, as well as movie and TV novelizations. Her books have been translated into twenty-four languages. The award-winning Nate the Great series, hailed in *Booklist* as "groundbreaking," has resulted in Nate's real-world appearances in many *New York Times* crossword puzzles, sporting a milk mustache in magazines and posters, residing on more than 28 million boxes of Cheerios, and touring the country in musical theater. Marjorie Weinman Sharmat and her husband, Mitchell Sharmat, have also coauthored many books, including titles in both the Nate the Great and the Olivia Sharp series.

MARC SIMONT won the Caldecott Medal for his artwork in *A Tree Is Nice* by Janice May Udry, as well as a Caldecott Honor for his own book, *The Stray Dog*. He illustrated the first twenty books in the Nate the Great series.